SOULSHADE ACADEMY

Laura Shenton

SOULSHADE ACADEMY

Laura Shenton

Iridescent Toad Publishing

Iridescent Toad Publishing.

Cover by Chan Cover Designs.

First edition. ISBN: 978-1-913779-46-7

Welcome to Soulshade Academy, where the ancient arts of witchcraft and spiritual energy converge to illuminate the path towards mastery and enlightenment; where the veil between worlds is thin, and the possibilities are endless.

Nestled amidst the shadows of towering trees and cloaked in an aura of mystique, Soulshade Academy stands as a beacon of knowledge and discovery for witches over the age of eighteen. Here, within the hallowed halls of our esteemed institution, students embark on a journey of self-discovery and transformation, guided by the wisdom of ages past and the boundless potential of their own innate abilities.

At Soulshade Academy, we understand that the pursuit of witchcraft is not merely a vocation, but a sacred calling – an eternal dance between the realms of the mundane and the mystical. Our curriculum is tailored to nurture and cultivate the natural talents of our students, many of whom possess a keen intuition and a profound connection to the spiritual energies that permeate the world around them.

Through a rigorous blend of theoretical study, practical application, and experiential learning, students at Soulshade Academy are empowered to unlock the full potential of their spiritual energies, honing their skills in harmonic communication with the spirits of both the natural world and the afterlife. Whether it be through the invocation of ancient rituals, or the channelling of elemental forces, our students learn to wield their powers with grace, wisdom, and reverence.

Soulshade Academy is more than just a school: it is a community, a sanctuary, and a home away from home for witches from all walks of life. Here, amidst the tranquil beauty of our sprawling campus and the camaraderie of fellow students, witches find solace, support, and inspiration as they embark on their individual paths towards enlightenment.

So, whether you are a seasoned practitioner seeking to deepen your understanding of the arcane arts, or a novice taking your first tentative steps into the realm of magic, we invite you to join us on a journey of discovery unlike any other.

Prologue

A cold gust of wind whipped through Skye's hair, chilling her to the bone. In the depths of the night, she found herself ensnared in the tendrils of a haunting dream, her subconscious enveloped in a swirling haze of emotions and memories. As she wandered through the labyrinth of shadows in her mind, her senses were heightened, albeit in a shroud of uncertainty.

The air was heavy with the scent of wildflowers and earth, carrying with it the faint echo of distant whispers and the rustle of unseen spirits. Above, the sky stretched out in an endless expanse of velvety darkness, punctuated only by the soft glow of distant stars that flickered like distant beacons in the night.

As Skye moved through the dream, she felt as though she was walking on the edge of reality, attuned to the subtle variances in the atmosphere around her. Shadows danced and shifted in the periphery of her vision, morphing into fantastical shapes and forms that seemed to pulse with an otherworldly life of their own.

In the distance, she could hear the sound of rushing water, the gentle murmur of a hidden stream that wound its way through the landscape like a silver ribbon. The melody of the water played in her ears, a soothing lullaby that beckoned her closer with its siren song.

Despite her looming sense of apprehension, Skye pressed on, driven by an unspoken instinct that urged her forward into the heart of the dream.

Suddenly, everything went black. The landscape dissolved into a void of impenetrable darkness, leaving Skye in an abyss so profound that even her hands became invisible. Panic gripped her like a vice, squeezing out every ounce of courage as she struggled to make sense of her surroundings.

"Skye," called a familiar voice, vivid, yet gentle as a summer breeze.

"Mum?" Skye responded in disbelief.

Skye reached out into the darkness with trembling hands, longing to embrace her mother, yearning to feel her warmth once again.

"Skye," repeated the voice of her mother, fainter now, as if drifting away like sand in the wind.

"Where are you?" Skye cried out, her bereavement pushing her forward, demanding answers. "I can't see you!"

"Skye, my darling," her mother's voice echoed softly.

Skye couldn't fight the feeling that something was terribly wrong. Why couldn't she see her mother?

"Please, Mum, let me see you!" she begged, frantically stepping further into the blackness. "Please."

"Skye…" said the voice, becoming more distant again.

Desperation clawed at Skye's chest, leaving her with an unbearable emptiness as she strained to hear her mother's voice.

"Mum, come back!" she shouted into the icy wind that swept around her.

Tears streamed down Skye's cheeks, but she refused to give up, her curiosity and determination unrelenting. She had to find her mother, even if it meant having to traverse this shadowy realm forever. The dream was so vivid, so real, that the thought of waking up felt like a betrayal. Skye knew that once she opened her eyes, her mother's voice would be lost to her, swallowed by the emptiness of reality. In this moment, holding on to the tenuous connection to her mother was all that mattered.

"Skye," said the soft voice once more, barely audible.

"Mum, please. I need you."

The silence that followed was deafening, a

heavy weight that settled over Skye like a suffocating blanket, smothering her in its cruel embrace. It stretched on, a yawning chasm of emptiness that threatened to swallow her whole.

She felt her resolve waver, her sense of isolation growing more acute with every passing second. The absence of her mother's voice left her feeling adrift in a sea of uncertainty, lost in a world where even her own thoughts seemed to betray her.

The darkness pressed in from all sides, closing in around Skye with a constricting intensity. It felt like a tangible force, crushing her spirit beneath its mass and leaving her feeling more alone than she had ever felt before.

She reached out blindly, searching for any sign of hope or salvation.

"Mum? Mum! Where are you? Please, come back!"

Chapter One

The underground library was a study in contrasts. Shadows and light danced together as the flickering of candle flames illuminated the towering shelves that seemed to stretch on forever.

Surrounded by silence, Skye sat alone at a solitary desk, encircled by rows of empty seats that seemed to stretch endlessly into the darkness.

Detention, she thought, shaking her head and causing her long sandy-blonde hair to ripple in small waves. *We're all adult witches who have chosen to study at Soulshade Academy. What do they think they're playing at, handing out detentions?!*

She sighed, and drummed her fingers against the rickety wooden desk, its surface marred with age. The cold air of the unpopulated space clung to her skin like a shroud, causing her to shiver slightly.

Oh well, she told herself, trying to suppress the lingering frustration. *I guess even an academy for adult witches needs to keep some kind of order.*

Despite the oppressive atmosphere that came with the library being used as a space for detention, there was a certain beauty to it. The scent of old leather and aged paper filled the air, while intricate ironwork spiralled around the supports that held up the vaulted ceiling. Compared to the rest of the academy, it felt like another world – one where secrets lay hidden just beneath the surface, waiting for someone to unearth them.

Skye wished that she could use the time to catch up on some reading, but deep down, something was gnawing away at her and she just couldn't focus. Besides, she was doing well in her studies and no such issue was the root cause of her current predicament.

It's not my fault I overslept. That dream... it was so vivid.

Her mind wandered back to the dream that had plagued her night with equal parts haunting uncertainty and inexplicable comfort as the soft echo of her mother's voice had called out to her.

In the dream, Skye had found herself suspended in a realm of shadows, unable to see her surroundings, but acutely aware of her mother's voice. Despite the unsettling nature of the dream, Skye hadn't been able to resist its pull. A part of her had longed to stay asleep, to linger in the liminal space, even if only in the confines of her mind.

And so, when the morning light had filtered through her window and beckoned her back to the waking world, Skye had already made a subconscious decision to stay asleep – intent on grasping at the threads of the dream and unravelling its mysteries, even if it meant facing the consequences of turning up late to class. In the fleeting moments between sleep and wakefulness, she had felt closer to her mother than she had in years, a bittersweet reminder of the love that transcended even the boundaries of life and death.

Perhaps it was nothing more than a jumbled mixture of memories and fears.

"Damn it," Skye muttered under her breath, frustrated with herself, but still unable to deny just how vivid the dream had been.

Mercifully, her train of thought was abruptly jolted back to reality by the unmistakable sound of shuffling footsteps. With a start, she looked up from the scratches on the wooden desk, surprised and awkward as she met the gaze of Casey, a student whose presence she had only glimpsed in passing.

Casey's eyes darted furtively around the library as she clutched an ancient-looking book tightly against her chest. With her long dark hair cascading in waves around her shoulders, and a mischievous smirk playing upon her lips, she exuded an aura of mystery that piqued Skye's interest.

"Hey," Casey said softly, glancing over at Skye before quickly scanning the towering shelves for any sign of teachers or other students. "You've got detention too, huh?"

"I overslept," Skye replied. "What about you?"

"I got caught with this beauty," Casey said as she affectionately patted the leather-bound tome in her arms. "It's a spell book that I picked up from the library in town. There's some really powerful stuff in here. But, of course, the dean confiscated it."

"I bet it makes for an interesting read," Skye said, intrigued by Casey's rebelliousness.

"Yeah," Casey said confidently, a proud grin on her face. "Soulshade Academy may be prestigious, but they're so damn uptight about sticking to their traditions. They don't want us learning any magic that they don't approve of."

"It does seem narrow-minded," Skye said thoughtfully, feeling a kinship with this rule-breaking witch.

"Exactly! I want to learn everything I possibly can, even if it's forbidden," said Casey, winking conspiratorially. "And anyway, the dean doesn't know that I made sure to learn a handy little spell from this book before he took it away."

"Really?" Skye asked, curious to hear more.

"Yeah," said Casey. "I was able to make the book materialise back in my hands as I made my way down here. Now I just need to find a good hiding spot for it."

"I'll help if you like," Skye said, alight with excitement. "I could use a distraction from going stir-crazy down here."

"Alright," said Casey. "And I'm trusting you not to tell anybody about this."

"I won't. I promise. You have my word."

"It's Skye, isn't it?" Casey asked.

"Yeah."

"I thought so," said Casey. "Even though we don't have any classes together, I've seen you around."

"I got here six months ago."

"Ah, ok. I'm in the second year."

Feeling comfortable in Casey's company and sensing that she could trust her, Skye helped to scour the dimly lit shelves of the underground library, searching for the perfect hiding place for the forbidden tome.

With practiced ease, Casey navigated the labyrinth of shelves, her fingers trailing along many different spines as she scanned for the perfect hiding place.

"This ought to do it," she said. "Nobody will think to look for a book on this part of the shelf. It's full of texts on how to do things the old-fashioned way."

"Good thinking," said Skye. "I can't think of a single witch here who would want to turn someone into a frog. It's too predictable."

"Right," Casey said with a chuckle.

With the contraband reliably concealed, Skye and Casey returned to their respective desks. Casey sat quietly, scanning the pages of a more innocuous-looking spell book, just in case a teacher decided to check up on them. Skye couldn't help but feel a little envious of her studious focus, especially when her own thoughts kept wandering back to the dream she'd had.

In an effort to distract herself, Skye sat back in her hard wooden chair, her gaze drifting over the rows of ancient books all around, their spines cracked and worn from centuries of use, and their musty scent dominating the space.

As a faint scratching noise reached her ears, her attention wavered.

"Casey," she whispered, her eyes narrowing with suspicion. "Can you hear that?"

"Hear what?" Casey asked, glancing up from her book.

"Listen," Skye said urgently, holding up a hand for silence, her brows furrowed in concentration.

The scratching sound persisted, growing louder and more insistent until it was accompanied by a soft mewling noise. Skye's heart clenched with worry, her instincts telling her that something was trapped and needed help.

"Casey," she said hastily, rising from her chair and heading towards the source of the noise.

"I think there's an animal stuck behind the wall. We need to get it out."

"Are you sure?" Casey asked, quickly leaving her desk to join Skye by the wall.

"Whatever it is, it sounds like it needs our help," Skye insisted, running her fingers over the worn bricks, searching for any sign of weakness.

"Alright, let's find a loose brick or something," Casey agreed, beginning her own examination of the wall.

They worked together, meticulously checking the small area for any indication of a way in.

"Here!" Skye exclaimed, her fingertips catching on a slightly protruding brick. "Help me pull this out."

"Ok," Casey responded, gripping the edge on the other end of the brick.

Wiggling and tugging at the brick, with their combined strength, they caused it to shift, revealing a small, dark cavity within the wall.

The mewling grew louder, more desperate, urging them to continue.

"Come on, we're almost there," Skye said, her voice strained with the effort as they removed another brick.

In a crumble of dust and rubble, the hole grew larger, and as another brick fell away, a pair of gleaming green eyes peered out from the darkness.

"No way!" Casey said breathily, her tone a blend of relief and astonishment. "It's a cat!"

Chapter Two

The cat emerged from the hole in the wall, confidently stretching its legs as it stepped into the dim light of the underground library. Skye couldn't help but be captivated by the sleek feline.

Mostly black with long fur, it had a striking symmetrical white mark spanning its nose and mouth, starkly contrasting against its ebony fur and accentuating its features.

As the cat gracefully took another step forward, the subtle surrounding light revealed glimpses of its pristine snowy-white underbelly. Each foot was adorned with a dainty white sock, while its slightly scraggly tail, also tipped in white, flicked with an air of mischief and intrigue.

"He's a beautiful boy," Casey murmured, still

crouched down by the hole in the wall and leaning in closer to get a better look at their unexpected discovery. "All things considered, he seems so calm."

Kneeling beside Casey, Skye smiled and nodded her head in agreement, her emotions swelling with a sudden protectiveness towards the cat. She carefully extended her hand, allowing him to sniff her fingers before she tentatively petted his head. To her delight, he leaned into her touch, purring softly in response.

"He seems very drawn to you," Casey observed, a hint of amusement in her voice. "I've never seen a cat take to someone so quickly."

"That's amazing," Skye replied, feeling a strange connection to the animal.

As she continued to stroke the cat, she couldn't help but notice how healthy and well-groomed he appeared to be, despite having been trapped behind the wall just moments ago.

"He looks perfectly fine, doesn't he?" she

asked. "Not hurt or anything?"

"I agree," said Casey, fascinated as she watched the cat's confident interaction with Skye.

"How do you think he ended up behind that wall? And how could he possibly have survived?" Skye questioned, her voice hesitant, but driven by her ever-growing curiosity.

"Honestly, I have no idea," Casey replied, her forehead creasing as she pondered the question. "It's baffling, really."

"Yeah," said Skye. "It seems… impossible. Like something out of a storybook."

"Maybe we should ask him," Casey suggested with a playful smirk. "Hey, Mr Cat, what's your story?"

The cat glanced up at Casey, blinking slowly before returning his attention to Skye and nudging her hand to demand more scratches behind his ears.

"Alright, alright, keep your secrets," Casey

said with a soft giggle, affectionately ruffling the cat's fur. "We'll figure it out eventually."

"Or maybe we won't," Skye said, her gaze thoughtful as she continued to stroke the cat. "Maybe some things are meant to remain mysteries."

"Like your strange affinity for this feline?" Casey teased affectionately.

"Perhaps," Skye replied, trying to sound serious, but unable to suppress a smile.

She looked down at the cat, his purr rumbling like a tiny motor. The connection was undeniable; it was as if the universe had placed them on a collision course destined to intertwine their lives.

"I think we should keep him a secret from everyone else," Casey said wisely. "He seems to have chosen you as his person. I'd hate to see anyone else around here trying to claim him as their own. You know what some witches can be like, especially when it comes to how badly some of them yearn for a familiar."

"Thanks," Skye said gratefully. "Admittedly, as much as I've always loved animals, I had always assumed that I could do without a familiar. Considering that this sweet little guy seems to have chosen me though, I'm all for it."

"I agree," said Casey, her tone sincere. "Your secret is safe with me."

"I'll do everything I can to look after him," said Skye. "I bet he's hungry – he must be starving after having been trapped behind that wall!"

She reached into her pocket and pulled out a crumbled cereal bar, breaking off a small piece. As she offered the morsel to the cat, he sniffed it delicately before taking a gentle nibble, purring his appreciation.

"I'm glad he likes it," said Skye, "but I thought he would be ravenous in the circumstances."

"Bless him," said Casey. "He's certainly a character!"

Skye found herself drawn to the cat's every movement, her gaze tracing the curve of his elegant form as he calmly savoured the crumbs. There was a certain tranquillity in the way he ate, a sense of contentment that seemed to radiate from his very being.

"Let's give him a drink," Casey said, getting up and walking to her desk to rummage in her bag. "He's probably thirsty."

"Good idea."

"Here you go," Casey said as she bent down to pass a bottle of water to Skye.

Skye unscrewed the cap and poured a small amount of water into it, setting it down beside the cat. Seeming to be in no rush, he calmly lapped up the water, and then yawned widely, displaying an impressive set of sharp teeth.

"Hey, Skye," Casey said suddenly, glancing up at the clock on the wall, "detention's almost over."

Skye looked around for something that she could safely and discreetly use to carry the cat in. Her eyes fell upon her purple velvet shoulder bag, adorned with appliqué yellow stars. It wasn't ideal, but it would have to do.

She rose to her feet and gently scooped the cat up in her arms, cradling him close to her chest.

"Here, kitty," she said softly as she carefully lowered him into the spacious confines of her bag.

The cat meowed softly, almost as if in understanding. He then curled up amidst the jumble of textbooks without protest, tucking his head beneath a soft fold of fabric.

Satisfied that the sweet feline was comfortable, Skye diligently folded the flap of the bag shut, leaving a small gap for air.

"Here, let me help you," Casey said kindly as she slowly eased the strap of the bag over Skye's shoulder.

"Thanks," said Skye.

Despite Skye's surprise at just how heavy her bag had become, the weight wasn't a burden. Instead, the warmth of the cat's presence radiated through the fabric, a tangible reminder of their connection.

Chapter Three

Following behind Casey, Skye ascended the steps out of the underground library. She could only hope that nobody would notice the cat in her bag. She couldn't bear the thought of him being taken away or put outside. Although she couldn't quite put her finger on it, and although they had only just met, her need to keep the cat with her was overwhelming.

Stay quiet, little one, she thought as she gently brushed her fingers over her bag.

Remarkably, the cat remained still and silent. It was as though he understood the situation entirely.

As they reached the top of the stairs, the door at ground level creaked open, causing Skye to squint as the light hit her.

"Evening, Professor," Casey said sincerely.

Keeping her arm over her bag, Skye looked up to meet the gaze of Professor Dumer. One of Soulshade's most esteemed members of staff, he had short-cropped salt-and-pepper hair, a square jaw, and piercing blue eyes that seemed to assess every detail before him. His expression was stern yet fair, as if challenging Casey and Skye to prove themselves worthy of his time.

"Skye Glover and Casey Wentworth," he greeted them in a steely voice. "I trust you've spent your detention time wisely."

"Of course, Professor," Skye replied, trying her best to sound neutral despite her anxiety.

She clutched her bag tightly, praying that the cat hidden within would remain unnoticed throughout this interaction.

"Very well," Professor Dumer said, opening the register in his hands with a flourish.

As he began to sign it, Skye couldn't help but hold her breath, her mind racing with potential excuses should he discover the feline stowaway.

"Done," Professor Dumer announced, snapping the book shut and looking back at them. "You're both free to go. Don't make a habit of this."

"Understood," Casey responded, not quite wholeheartedly, but convincing enough.

"Thanks, Professor," said Skye, keen to get moving.

As the two witches made their way through the quiet corridors of the academy, the soft glow of lanterns cast flickering shadows upon the high walls, creating a soothing atmosphere despite their predicament. The silence that enveloped them was broken only by the sound of their footsteps. In the late hour, the corridors were nearly deserted, much to Skye's relief.

She was looking forward to reaching the privacy of her dorm room. Only then would she be able to let her guard down entirely. Not only that, but she was sure the cat would be more comfortable on her bed.

Casey walked with a casual ease, seeming to be more relaxed in her demeanour. Every so often, she glanced at Skye's bag in a silent acknowledgment of the secret they both carried. Though their paths had rarely crossed before tonight, there was now a sense of camaraderie between them.

As they reached the junction where their paths would diverge, Skye offered a grateful smile to Casey.

"Thanks again," she said.

"You're more than welcome," said Casey. "Best detention I've ever had!"

Skye couldn't help but chuckle softly, and with that, they parted ways.

As Skye headed down the hallways towards her own dorm room, her thoughts were consumed by the incredible bond she felt with the enigmatic feline hidden in her bag. She was amazed at how still and quiet he had been during their encounter with Professor Dumer. It was almost as if the cat understood the importance of remaining unnoticed – a remarkable feat for any animal, let alone a feline who could have easily scarpered in fear.

"Seems like you knew what was at stake, huh?" Skye whispered to the bag, a small smile playing on her lips. "Or maybe I'm just lucky."

The cat stirred slightly, as though acknowledging her words. She couldn't deny the powerful connection she felt. The cat had chosen her, and she intended to do everything in her power to protect and nurture that bond.

Ever-mindful of the precious cargo hidden in her bag, Skye turned a corner. Her face fell at the sight before her. Standing at their lockers were two of her least favourite people: Constance and Marissa.

Skye's eyes flicked from one sneering face to another, taking in the witches' smirking expressions and the way they stood with their arms folded. Like Skye and Casey, Constance and Marissa were both in their early twenties, but carried themselves with an arrogance that belied their abilities. They were attractive, no doubt – Constance with her long golden curls and ice-blue eyes, Marissa with her flowing raven-black hair framing her sharp features like a dark halo – but their beauty was marred by the cruelty that radiated from them. The pair were known for their love of tormenting others, with Constance as the ringleader and Marissa her loyal sidekick.

"Detention for oversleeping, Skye?" Constance taunted. "What a baby! Next we'll be hearing that you pissed the bed."

Skye gritted her teeth, her grip on her bag tightening. She couldn't let them see how much they got under her skin – especially when getting the cat back to her room unnoticed was the priority right now.

"I'm doing just fine, thanks," she shot back, the words tasting bitter on her tongue.

"Really?" Marissa chimed in, her voice dripping with disdain. "You could have fooled us."

The cat shifted slightly in Skye's bag. She tensed, praying that he wouldn't make a sound. She needed to defuse the situation and get away before something could go wrong.

"To be honest with you both," she said tactically, "I'm feeling a bit sick. I'd love to stop and chat, but I need to get to the loo."

Pleased with herself for her quick thinking, Skye walked hastily away. She was feeling completely fine save for the need to get the cat up to her room.

"See you around, loser," Constance called out after her, cackling as Skye disappeared around a corner.

God, I hate them, Skye thought. As much as she wanted to curse their names and plot her revenge though, she knew she had more pressing matters to attend to. The cat hidden in her bag was a secret she needed to protect at all costs. Mercifully, he had remained silent throughout the entire encounter.

"Thank you," she whispered into the fabric of her bag, relief washing over her. "You have no idea how much trouble you saved me from."

She felt a nudge against her side, as though the cat understood her gratitude and was reassuring her in return.

Ok, just a few more minutes and we'll be safe, she told herself, the tension in her shoulders gradually easing. As she rounded one last corner, the familiar sight of the door to her room finally came into view.

Chapter Four

As Skye stepped into her dorm room, a wave of relief washed over her as she closed and locked the door behind her, turning her back on the outside world and sealing herself within the soothing embrace of her sanctuary.

As a matter of priority, she gently placed her bag on her queen-sized bed, which she hadn't made due to having been in a rush earlier that day. Figuring that the cat would be most comfortable on the mattress amongst the plush pillows and duvet set, she slowly lifted the flap on her bag so as not to alarm him.

"Welcome home," she said softly. "Come out whenever you're ready."

With a delicate rustle of fabric, the feline

emerged from the depths of the bag, his movements fluid and graceful as he stretched his limbs and arched his back in a display of confidence. Giving a satisfied purr, he settled into a more comfortable position upon the bed, his sleek form sinking into the messy mound of duvet with a sense of ease. As he nestled into the soft folds of material, his eyes gleamed with a quiet intelligence, seemingly a silent acknowledgment of his newfound freedom within the confines of Skye's dorm room.

"I hope you'll be happy here," she said. "Oh, and sorry about the mess. I can't say I'm the tidiest person to live with, but I'll do my best for you."

Filled with personal touches, Skye's room was a cosy space. Books lay scattered across her desk, and various trinkets and charms adorned the walls. Their corners slightly curled with age, posters of famous witches hung haphazardly. In one corner of the room stood a small wardrobe, its door slightly ajar, revealing an array of outfits that hadn't quite been hung up properly on their hangers. A large window opposite Skye's bed allowed the soft evening light to filter through, casting long shadows across the carpets laid upon the wooden flooring.

"I'm going to take a quick shower," she told the cat, feeling the grime of the underground library clinging to her skin. "You just make yourself at home, ok?"

The cat blinked slowly in response, seemingly content with the current arrangement. With a nod, Skye retreated to her en-suite.

As she stood in the shower, hot water cascaded down her tense shoulders, soothing her tired muscles. The steam enveloped her in a cocoon, allowing her a precious moment of peace. She tilted her head back, letting the shower rain down on her as she took a deep, calming breath.

This feels good, she thought, running her fingers through her tangled hair.

As the hot water continued to work its magic, Skye couldn't help but let her thoughts drift back to the dream that had caused her to oversleep. She could still hear her mother's voice as though it was echoing through the steam around her – haunting yet comforting.

"Skye… Skye," the familiar voice rang out.

"Mum?" Skye whispered, her heart aching with a mixture of longing and fear. "Where are you?"

"Skye…" the voice said, quickly fading into the ether and leaving her feeling more alone than ever.

Damn it! Skye thought, frustration threatening to overwhelm her.

She could still remember the devastating news of her mother's car accident – a cruel reminder that witches were not immortal. The idea that her mother was simply gone forever still didn't sit right with her. Skye had been grieving the loss since the age of eight, and years later, every so often, she would find herself experiencing a fresh wave of sadness.

Was it more than just a dream? Skye wondered. *Or am I just looking for some kind of connection because I miss her so much?*

The water continued to rain down on her,

offering no answers or clarity. Skye found herself lingering in the shower, hoping to recapture even a whisper of her mother's voice. She knew she couldn't stay there forever – not with her newfound feline friend waiting for her – but it felt good to stand under the water, letting her thoughts drift.

Maybe the cat's a sign, she mused. *Or perhaps I'm just overthinking things... as usual.*

With a sigh, she gave her hair a final rinse, and then turned off the water. She stepped out of the shower, wrapping herself in a fluffy towel.

She looked in the mirror, steam clinging to it and blurring her reflection. The hot water had relaxed her muscles and washed away the grime of the underground library, but it hadn't been enough to cleanse her mind of the haunting dream. Her mother's voice, so close yet so distant, played over in her head like a broken record.

Perhaps my mind is playing tricks on me, she pondered as she towelled her hair dry.

She wished she could confide in one of the academy's teachers; perhaps they would be able to shed some light on the whole thing. However, the personal nature of her question was such that just the thought of sharing it with anyone made her uncomfortable.

Discarding the towel, she pulled on her pyjamas. She didn't want to leave the black cat unattended for too long. It was still a small miracle that he had remained hidden and quiet during their journey from the underground library.

Back in the room, Skye was pleased to see the cat curled up on the end of her bed. His soft purring filled her ears like a gentle lullaby as she settled onto the mattress and pulled the duvet up to her chin.

As she shifted in her bed, trying to find the most comfortable position, she knew that a good night's rest would be essential in order to avoid another detention for oversleeping. A part of her still couldn't shake the lingering thoughts of her mother and the strange dream she'd had, but now was not the time to dwell on it; she needed to settle down.

As she lay there, she couldn't help but reflect on the day's events and how serendipitous it was that she had found the cat. Somehow, the creature seemed to understand her, to accept her, even though they had only known each other for a few hours.

"Maybe you're my guardian angel, huh?" she murmured. "Here to help me figure out what's going on?"

The cat let out a long purring sound, as if in acknowledgement of Skye's words.

"Or maybe I'm just overtired and imagining things," she said softly.

The cat's purring grew louder and more soothing as he moved to snuggle deep beneath the duvet.

"Either way, I'm glad you're here," Skye murmured, feeling her eyelids getting heavier by the second.

The warmth of the cat's body against her legs was oddly reassuring, grounding her in a way that she hadn't felt in a long time. It was as though he wanted to protect her from any lingering shadows.

"Goodnight," she whispered, finally allowing herself to drift off to sleep.

Chapter Five

Sunlight crept through the gap in Skye's curtains, casting a golden haze across her room. With a contented sigh, she stretched beneath the warm duvet, feeling refreshed and alert. Compared to the night before, she had slept so well. A feeling of relief washed over her as she realised that she hadn't been plagued by the distressing dream.

At the end of her bed, under the covers, she could feel the comforting weight and warmth of the cat.

"Good morning," she whispered, her voice still thick with sleep.

She was careful not to startle him as she peeled back the duvet and reached out to stroke the soft fur on his back.

He nuzzled against her hand, purring sweetly. She felt grateful for the sense of serenity he seemed to bring.

Giving the cat one last affectionate pat and then swinging her legs over the side of the bed, Skye glanced around her room, thinking about how important it was to keep her new companion hidden from not just the staff, but the other students.

"Let's get you some breakfast, shall we?"

She padded quietly across her room to rummage through her messy drawers, searching for something that would be suitable for the unexpected guest.

"Ah, perfect!" she exclaimed softly, spotting a can of tuna hidden amongst several pots of instant noodles and packets of crisps.

She grabbed two bowls – one for the fish and another for water – and hurried back to the cat, who watched her every move with a curious expression.

She opened the can of tuna and emptied its contents into one of the bowls, setting it down beside the bed. She then filled the second bowl with water and placed it nearby.

"Here you go," she said. "I hope you like it."

The cat didn't hesitate to jump down from his spot on the bed to investigate the offering. In no time at all, he started on the flaky fish.

As Skye watched him eat, he seemed content, which only fuelled her desire to protect him from prying eyes. She knew that keeping a secret pet in her dorm room would be difficult, but not necessarily impossible.

"I'll keep you safe. I promise."

The cat looked up from his meal for a moment, meeting Skye's gaze in what she interpreted as a silent acknowledgment of their clandestine arrangement.

"I'm so glad I only have one class this morning," she said, her voice tinged with satisfaction as she began to rummage through her belongings, gathering her books and supplies. "I'll make sure to leave you plenty of water."

Confident that the cat would be safe and at ease in her dorm room while she was away, Skye reasoned that leaving him alone for a few hours would be the best way to keep him a secret.

Discarding her pyjamas in a crumpled pile on the floor, she slipped into her short-sleeved dark checked shirt, the soft fabric clinging to her frame with familiarity. She then put on her black pinafore dress, the smooth material draping elegantly over her figure. Its simple-yet-classic design was a testament to the timeless elegance of the academy's dress code, a uniform that spoke of tradition and discipline.

Next, she reached for her black tie, looping it neatly around her collar with practiced ease. As she adjusted the knot, her reflection in the mirror stared back at her with a sense of determination, her gaze unwavering as she prepared to face the day ahead.

As she pulled on her sheer black tights and smart black shoes, Skye couldn't help but feel a sense of pride in her appearance. The uniform was more than just clothing; it was a symbol of her commitment to her studies.

Although she had been late for class yesterday due to having overslept, she, like every other witch at Soulshade Academy, was there through her own choice.

Skye then turned her attention to her bag. She smiled as she picked it up and put some books inside, recalling how just last night, the cat had been nestled in the same spot.

"I'm gonna head off now," she said, bending down to give the cat a quick scratch behind his ears. "Be good while I'm gone. I'll be back soon."

As she made her way to the door, she felt the weight of responsibility lifting slightly from her shoulders. It was comforting to know that even though she couldn't be with the cat all the time, he would be safe in her absence. With a final glance back at her feline companion, she stepped out into the hallway, closing the door quietly behind her.

Chapter Six

As Skye stepped into the classroom for her first and only lesson of the day, she was immediately welcomed by the faint scent of incense and herbs. The walls were adorned with tapestries depicting intricate sigils and symbols. Beneath them, were display tables of crystals, and candles, their flickering flames casting dancing shadows upon the walls and infusing the space with a soft, ethereal glow. At the front of the room, a large chalkboard stood covered in diagrams and notes.

"Good morning, Poppy," Skye said to her classmate as she took a seat at their desk.

"Morning, Skye," Poppy greeted with a cheerful grin, her long black hair framing the pretty apples of her cheeks. "You look more alert than usual."

"Thanks, I had a good night's sleep," Skye replied, refusing to elaborate.

I can't tell anyone about the cat. Poppy is alright, but there are others who would probably try to take him away from me, despite our connection.

As if on cue, Constance and Marissa sauntered into the room, their laughter echoing off the walls. They took their seats directly behind Skye and Poppy, and immediately began their cruel commentary.

"Ooh, look who's bothered to show up today!" Constance mocked loudly, just out of Skye's line of sight.

"I'm impressed that she found her way to class," Marissa chimed in, snickering maliciously. "She always looks so lost."

Skye clenched her fists under the desk, her nails biting into her palms. The urge to retaliate was overwhelming, but she knew better than to give them the satisfaction. Fortunately, the door creaked open and the class teacher walked in with an air of authority.

"Good morning, everyone!" Miss Lumos greeted, her voice silencing the room.

Her red hair cascading down her shoulders like a waterfall of flames, Miss Lumos' emerald-green eyes sparkled with enthusiasm. Skye couldn't help but admire her stylish attire: a flowing black dress adorned with intricate silver embroidery, coupled with knee-high leather boots that hinted at both elegance and power.

"Today," Miss Lumos announced, her melodic voice captivating every student in the room, "we will be exploring how to achieve harmony with nature. As witches of Soulshade Academy, it is vital that we understand the delicate balance between our own energies and those of the natural world."

Skye leaned forward in her seat, her interest piqued. She glanced around the room and noticed that even Constance and Marissa were paying intense attention to Miss Lumos, their usual arrogance momentarily tempered.

"Harmony is not just about physical balance," Miss Lumos continued, her voice soft yet commanding. "It encompasses a deeper connection, a spiritual harmony that transcends our mundane existence. It is this harmony that allows us to tap into the full potential of our magical abilities."

As a murmur of fascination rippled through the classroom, Skye felt a shiver of excitement coursing through her veins. This was precisely the kind of knowledge she craved – something beyond the rote memorisation of spells and incantations that other academies were renowned for.

"Remember," Miss Lumos said, her eyes sweeping across the room, locking onto each student's gaze for a brief moment, "the path to true harmony requires dedication, patience, and a willingness to listen – not just to the whispers of the earth, but to the silent call of our own souls."

Skye's mind raced with questions and possibilities. How could she forge this deeper connection to nature? What untapped potential lay dormant within her, waiting to be awakened?

Is this the kind of thing that could help me to

understand that dream I had?

Skye took a deep breath and turned her full attention back to Miss Lumos, determined to absorb every word of wisdom the popular teacher had to offer.

"By attuning ourselves to the natural world, we can gain a deeper insight into our own magical abilities," Miss Lumos explained. "Once you've found that balance, you'll be able to channel your powers more effectively and efficiently. And of course, you can only achieve that if you practice mindfulness and patience. Think of them as the keys you will need to unlock the door to true harmony."

I wonder if Miss Lumos could help me to understand that dream. I'm still not ready to talk to anyone about it yet – if at all! But if I absolutely had to ask someone about it, it would probably be her.

Though Skye wanted to remain wholly absorbed in the lesson, thoughts of her dream, and a nagging concern for the cat's wellbeing, lurked in the back of her mind like a persistent shadow. She hoped he was doing ok, waiting patiently for her return.

As the lesson drew to a close, Miss Lumos flashed a warm smile at the class.

"I know that today's topic is a lot to take in," she said. "I know it's incredibly abstract, but trust yourselves – and the process. You're all capable of achieving great things."

Already gathering her belongings, Skye slung her bag over her shoulder and hurriedly made her way out of the classroom. She then dashed through the halls of the academy, keen to get back to her room.

***

Skye barged into her room, revealing the cosy space bathed in the warm late-morning sunlight. A sense of relief washed over her as she spotted the cat curled up on her bed, his fur shimmering like midnight velvet. For a moment, she allowed herself to bask in the serene sight, grateful for the unexpected companionship that had found its way into her life.

"Hey," she whispered, locking the door behind her and then approaching the cat to stroke his soft fur. "I'm glad you're ok."

He stretched languidly, purring contentedly beneath her touch.

With her newfound friend safe and sound, Skye turned her thoughts to stocking up on supplies for him. With no afternoon classes on her timetable, it would buy her just enough time to slip away from the academy to gather everything she would need.

As she rummaged through her drawers for a snack, her fingers brushing against an unopened bag of crisps, her attention was suddenly drawn to the sound of paper sliding across the floor. She turned around to find that a neatly-folded note had been pushed under her door.

What could that be?

She abandoned her search for sustenance in favour of retrieving the mysterious message. As she unfolded the crisp white paper, her heart sank.

"Room inspections tomorrow," she muttered, feeling the blood drain from her face as she read the words typed in bold font. "No! No, no, no! This complicates things so much!"

She glanced at the cat, who was still on her bed, relaxed and blissfully unaware of the predicament they now faced.

"Damn it," she said under her breath. "This is going to be tricky."

She knew that keeping the cat hidden during the inspection would be impossible if he remained in her dorm room. A plan began to form in her mind; she would have to take him to class with her, tucked away safely in her bag.

"I'm going to need a big favour from you tomorrow," she said softly as she ran her hand through the cat's silky fur. "Do you think you can stay hidden in my bag all day if I keep you with me?"

The cat looked up at her, his captivating viridian eyes filled with understanding and trust. It was as if he could sense her desperation. He rubbed his head against her hand, purring with affection.

"Alright then," she said, her tone full of gratitude. "Tomorrow, you'll be coming with me on a little mystery tour. I know it's not ideal, but you'll be safe with me."

Chapter Seven

The following morning, Skye awoke to the comforting weight of the cat nestled against her legs. She stretched, realising with a start that for the second night in a row, she hadn't been plagued by the distressing dream. The connection between the cat's presence and her newfound peace of mind was undeniably intriguing, though she couldn't quite put her finger on why.

"Good morning," she greeted the cat, bending forward to scratch behind his ears. "I hope you feel ready for our little adventure today."

He purred in response, nuzzling her adoringly. Skye smiled, feeling a strange sense of camaraderie with the mysterious feline. It was unlike anything she had ever experienced before.

"Ok," she said, full of determination. "Let's do this."

After a trip to the local store the previous afternoon, Skye had managed to stock up on some essentials. As she reached for a tin of cat food, the creature stretched out on the bed, his bright green eyes meeting hers.

When Skye pulled the ring on the can, the sound of the metal lid snapping open was met with an eager purr from the cat, who jumped down from the bed and wound himself around her legs.

"Alright, alright, just give me a second," she said with a chuckle as she bent down to empty the humble meal into a small bowl.

She then filled another bowl with fresh water, watching as the cat eagerly consumed his food.

With a contented sigh, Skye surveyed her room, noticing a small pile of cat poop in one corner. Though she'd expected some mess, she couldn't help but wrinkle her nose at the sight. She quickly grabbed a tissue and carefully scooped up the offending matter.

Then, with her hand outstretched, she made her way to the ensuite and flushed the waste away before washing her hands thoroughly.

As the cat lapped up the last remnants of his breakfast, Skye's thoughts turned to the day ahead. She knew it would be risky to take the cat to class with her, but the thought of leaving him alone for the caretaker to find was even more daunting.

She glanced around her room, taking in the cluttered mess that she had accumulated over time. She knew she would need to have a quick tidy-up in order to pass the impending room inspection.

"Alright," she muttered under her breath, rolling up her pyjama sleeves. "Time to make this place inspection-worthy."

She began by tidying her desk, shoving crumpled pieces of paper into drawers and stacking textbooks neatly in one corner. Her satisfaction faded, however, when she caught sight of the tins of cat food sitting conspicuously on her shelf. Panic rose in her chest as she realised they would be a dead giveaway during the inspection.

She grabbed a plastic bag from her desk drawer and quickly began stuffing the cans inside. She then scanned the room for a suitable hiding place, finally deciding that the back of the wardrobe, behind her clothes, would be her best bet.

Still anxious about her strategy, but with no other option, she tucked the bag of tins out of sight, praying that the caretaker wouldn't find them.

Acutely aware of the time, she quickly donned her dark checked shirt, black tie, and pinafore dress. She then pulled on her sheer black tights and slipped into her smart black shoes, the familiar weight of her uniform settling around her like armour.

"Ok," she said to the cat as she bent down to run a gentle hand through his soft fur. "Remember that you'll have to stay hidden in my bag until we get back. I promise to look after you. I've even put an old t-shirt in there to make it extra comfortable for you."

Worried that even her best efforts in the circumstances would seem feeble to the sweet cat, Skye held her breath, expecting some form of resistance – or disappointment. She was, after all, asking for quite a lot.

Instead, he gazed back at her with an air of understanding, almost as if genuinely acknowledging her words. For a moment, Skye was struck by his intelligence, wondering just how much of their secret arrangement he truly comprehended.

"Alright then, in you go," she said, placing her purple velvet bag in front of him as she opened the flap and gestured for him to climb in.

To her amazement, he stretched, and then calmly padded forward to settle into the soft confines of the bag without hesitation. Given the potential risks of the plan, Skye considered his trust both heartwarming and slightly unnerving. As she folded the bag shut, leaving a small gap for air just as she had done before, her mind raced. She had a full day of classes ahead and she wouldn't be able to go back to her room for lunch in case she was unlucky enough to bump into the caretaker. There was no scope for being able to let the cat out anywhere today for even the shortest interval.

Despite her worries though, Skye was convinced she was doing the right thing in having chosen to keep the cat a secret from everyone. She knew from past experiences that the academy was in the habit of making it their business when it came to deciding who was worthy of a familiar. She was certain that despite her strong bond with the cat, unscrupulous witches like Constance and Marissa would surely go out of their way to try and charm the creature for themselves if one of them wanted him badly enough.

I've never particularly yearned for a familiar, but ever since I found you behind the wall that day, I couldn't bear the thought of not keeping you around.

Skye smiled to herself then – both at the memory of having met the wonderful feline, and at how Casey had been so supportive and encouraging that he should be hers.

Deciding that now was not the time to dwell on things, Skye diligently put the bag over her shoulder with extra care, feeling the reassuring weight of the cat nestled inside.

Please let this work, she thought as she took

one last look around her room, doing a final check for any telltale giveaways as her heart pounded in anticipation.

"Remember, not a peep, ok?" she murmured softly into the bag.

A surge of protectiveness washed over her as she made her way to class, dedicated to keeping her companion comfortable and concealed from prying eyes.

Chapter Eight

With her hand protectively over her bag, Skye took a deep breath and entered the classroom. The warm glow of the morning light streamed in through the tall windows, casting a golden hue on the rows of worn wooden desks. She hurried to take her usual seat next to Poppy, and as she sat down, she gingerly placed her bag at her feet, ensuring that the cat could settle comfortably between her ankles.

"Hey, Skye!" Poppy greeted cheerfully, her eyes sparkling with curiosity. "You look ever so worried. What's up?"

"Nothing, really," Skye replied, doing her best to appear nonchalant as she smiled and brushed a strand of her long hair behind her ear. "I just had some terrible indigestion earlier."

"I guess you got up late and wolfed your breakfast down in a hurry," Poppy said kindly.

"You're probably right there," Skye lied.

She was grateful for the distraction when Miss Lumos breezed into the classroom with her usual flair, her charisma alone drawing attention from every student in the room.

With her perfectly styled flame-red hair, the popular teacher was dressed in a fashionable ensemble. Her fitted blazer, a deep shade of midnight blue, hugged her figure with tailored precision, accentuating her frame. The lapels were adorned with delicate moon-and-star-shaped brooches, each one sparkling in the sunlight. Beneath the blazer, she wore a flowing blouse in a soft lavender hue, its billowing sleeves catching the light as she moved. Her skirt, a sleek pencil silhouette in a rich velvet fabric, hugged her curves with understated sophistication. Completing the ensemble was a pair of stylish ankle boots with pointed toes and stiletto heels.

Skye couldn't help but admire the confidence with which Miss Lumos carried herself – a trait she wished she had more of herself.

Perhaps I wouldn't even need to keep the cat a secret if I was more assertive and better at sticking up for myself.

"Good morning, class," Miss Lumos greeted them with a warm smile. "Today, we'll be diving deeper into elemental alignments and their significance in our craft."

As much as Skye wanted to keep her focus on the lesson, her thoughts kept drifting towards the cat hidden in her bag. She hoped he was comfortable in there.

"Fire represents passion, creativity, and transformation," Miss Lumos continued, her voice captivating the room. "Air signifies communication, intellect, and clarity of thought."

Skye's senses heightened as she felt a faint shift in movement at her feet. She glanced down, her breath hitching when she saw the cat slipping out of her bag, purring contentedly as he settled again, no longer concealed.

"No!" she whispered urgently, panic surging through her.

"Skye?" Poppy whispered, concerned by her friend's sudden change in demeanour. "Are you ok?"

"Nothing, I just..." Skye trailed off, not wanting to draw attention to the situation. "I dropped my pen."

She bent down, pretending to pick up an imaginary writing instrument whilst attempting to coax the cat back into her bag. Despite her haste, he seemed unbothered, happily swishing his tail and refusing to hide.

"Remember, balance is key when working with the elements," Miss Lumos emphasised, her gaze sweeping across the room.

Skye held her breath, praying that nobody would notice the cat sitting at her feet. As she bit down on her lip, she was torn between the urge to listen to her favourite teacher and the pressing need to get the cat back into her bag.

"Psst," she hissed, reaching down to nudge him gently.

The cat merely stretched, unhurriedly flexing his claws in a way that made Skye wince. He then settled right back at her feet, his eyes gleaming with feline mischief.

Skye glanced frenziedly around the room, silently pleading that no one else had noticed the cat. She could see Constance and Marissa smirking behind their books. Her stomach clenched with dread at the thought of them discovering her secret.

Suddenly, with a graceful leap, the cat emerged from beneath the table, stretching his body across the floor like a shadow come to life. Skye's panic spiked, her pulse thundering in her ears as she watched him saunter towards the front of the class.

As if sensing her distress, the cat halted mid-stride, turning his head to cast her a cool, inscrutable stare. It was almost as though he was telling her not to worry, that he had everything under control.

"Skye," Miss Lumos said suddenly, causing Skye's heart to jump. "Can you tell me how you would approach combining the elements of fire and water?"

"Uh... yes," Skye stammered, trying to shift her focus back to the lesson. "You would need to find a balance between the two, perhaps by using steam as a medium."

"Very good," Miss Lumos replied, nodding approvingly. "Remember: an understanding of such harmony is imperative for anyone aspiring to master elemental magic."

She hasn't noticed him yet! How can that be?!

Skye's panic heightened as the cat began to weave his way through the legs of desks and chairs. She could almost feel a tangible wave of tension rolling on her skin, her palms slick with sweat as she gripped the edge of her desk. Her eyes flicked from the cat to her classmates, trying to discern if anyone else had noticed the feline intruder.

Are they blind?! Or am I going crazy?

The cat was now sitting directly in front of Miss Lumos, his tail flicking lazily as he gazed up at her with a curious tilt of his head.

Surely somebody can see him?!

"Look at that spider over there," Skye whispered to Poppy, nodding towards the wall closest to the cat.

"Oh," Poppy replied, squinting at the wall. "I can't see it."

Skye forced an uneasy smile as she glanced at the cat, still unseen by everyone else. The confirmation of its invisibility to others sent a chill down her spine.

As soon as the bell rang to signal the end of the lesson, Skye quickly gathered her things. She felt a weight settle in her bag as the cat climbed back inside. Relief washed over her that she could now take him with her, but overall, the feeling was tainted by what had just happened.

With her bag clutched tightly to her side, she hurried out of the classroom and made a beeline for the nearest restroom, her mind racing with questions and confusion. Once inside, she locked herself in a cubicle and took a deep breath, trying to calm down.

Ok, Skye... get a grip, she told herself, sitting down on the cold porcelain of the closed toilet seat. *This can't be real. Cats don't just turn invisible.*

Her bag, which she had placed on her lap, shifted slightly, reminding her of the very real presence inside. She knew she wasn't imagining things; the cat was there, and no one else in the classroom had seen him. But why?

"Damn it," she muttered under her breath, her frustration building. "Why does everything have to be so hard?"

As she sat there, trying to make sense of the situation, a sudden thought struck her.

Casey! She saw the cat when we first found him behind that wall in the underground library.

"Casey saw you too," she murmured to the cat, the words sounding hollow in the cramped cubicle. "I'm not going crazy."

Skye knew that if anyone could shed some light on this bizarre situation, it would be her fellow witch from the year above. Although they weren't close friends, there was an unspoken bond between them – a shared rebellious streak and insatiable curiosity. Besides, Casey was the one who had told Skye that she should keep the cat – and she'd promised Skye that she wouldn't tell anyone about him.

"Alright, little one," she whispered, determination seeping into her voice. "We need to find Casey."

Chapter Nine

Skye glanced at her watch, her eyes widening as she realised she'd been hiding in the toilet cubicle for nearly the length of a whole lesson. She knew that strolling in late would only land her in more trouble, and she couldn't afford another detention right now.

The notice board with all the class timetables... she thought with a mixture of nerves and commitment. *I need to find out where Casey is. I'll stay in here until everyone moves to their next class.*

Although the plan wasn't ideal, Skye knew it would be her best chance of being able to find Casey without drawing attention to herself. If any of the teachers found her walking the corridors during class time, it would be a dead giveaway that she wasn't where she was supposed to be.

Finally, the bell echoed through the halls like a siren, signalling the mass exodus of students from their classrooms. Skye braced herself, taking in a deep breath as she prepared to face the swarm. She then whispered a plea to the cat nestled in her bag.

"Stay put, *please.*"

She left the small cubicle and then pulled open the restroom door, just enough to slip out into the chaos. The cacophony of voices and footsteps filled her ears, heightening her anxiety. As she navigated through the crowd, she held her bag securely against her side, careful not to jostle its precious cargo.

Several corridors later, as she turned a corner, Skye finally spotted the notice board. Adorned with sheets of paper, it listed the various schedules of the academy's students. Her pulse quickened as she approached, hoping she could quickly locate Casey's class without attracting attention.

She frantically scanned the sheets for Casey's name, her eyes flicking back and forth with a sense of urgency.

There she is! Casey Wentworth... she's in the second division of the second year.

Feeling beads of sweat forming on her forehead, Skye looked for the corresponding class timetable. Thankful when she finally spotted it, she squinted at the schedule, making a mental note that Casey was currently on her way to a class called Roots to Branches: Elements in the Wood. A trickle of relief washed over her; at least now she had a destination.

I'll wait for Casey outside the classroom. I'll make sure I'm there for when she comes out.

For a moment, Skye considered attending her own next class, but quickly dismissed the idea. After what had happened in Miss Lumos' class, she couldn't bear the thought of missing the opportunity to talk to Casey. It felt far too risky to venture to the opposite end of the academy building. With a sigh, she decided her best bet would be to hide in the toilet cubicle closest to Casey's class until just before the end of lesson time.

Better safe than sorry, she reasoned, adjusting the strap of her bag on her shoulder and setting off down the corridor.

As she navigated the hallways of the academy, which were becoming less populated as more students got to their classes, Skye couldn't help but feel a pang of guilt for skipping yet another lesson. The uncomfortable feeling settled over her, a nagging voice in the back of her mind chastising her.

With a shake of her head and with determination setting her jaw, she then pushed aside the guilt that threatened to consume her, focusing instead on the task at hand. She reminded herself that sometimes, priorities shifted, and that right now, uncovering the truth about the cat in her bag was more important than everything else.

Forty-five minutes, she thought, checking her watch as she slipped into the restroom and locked herself in a cubicle. *Forty-five minutes to wait, and then I can finally talk to Casey. If anyone can help me to figure this out, it's her.*

As the minutes ticked by, Skye's breathing gradually returned to normal, her pulse steadying in the quiet sanctuary of the restroom.

Chapter Ten

The sound of the bell reverberated through the academy, signalling the end of lesson time. Skye flung the cubicle door open and sprinted towards Casey's classroom. Time seemed to slow down as she rounded the corner, her breath coming out in ragged gasps as she searched for any sign of the older witch.

I hope I'm not too late, she thought desperately.

Just as Skye skidded to a halt outside the classroom, Casey emerged, her sleek black hair swinging behind her as she raised an eyebrow at Skye.

"Skye, you look flustered," she remarked, her expression full of concern. "Are you ok?"

"Casey," Skye said, panting and trying to catch her breath. "I need to talk to you, but not here. It's about... you know."

"Ah, our little secret," Casey replied, her tone turning serious. "Alright, let's find somewhere private. How about we skip going to the canteen for lunch and head straight for the underground library. We can talk freely there."

"Are you sure?" Skye asked hesitantly.

"Trust me," Casey reassured, her voice filled with confidence. "Hardly anyone ever goes down there unless they've got detention. Besides, who would want to spend their free time in a place that smells like old books and damp?"

Skye couldn't help but chuckle at Casey's description. It was true; despite being a treasure trove of ancient knowledge, the underground library had an unappealing aroma that most students avoided.

"Alright," Skye agreed, figuring that there was nowhere else they could go for privacy during lunchtime.

"Perfect!" Casey said, clapping her hands together. "Let's go!"

Together, they made their way through the academy's winding corridors, careful not to draw attention to themselves. With each step, Skye felt a stark blend of anxiety and anticipation as they neared their destination.

The shadows seemed to dance on the walls as they descended the stairs into the darkness of the underground library. Skye clutched her bag tightly, feeling the soft purr of the black cat within. She glanced at Casey, whose eyes gleamed with a mixture of curiosity and concern.

"See?" Casey whispered, gesturing around the dimly lit space. "I told you there would be nobody here."

"Except for her," Skye murmured, nodding in the direction of an occupied table in the shadows.

A young witch was sitting there, hunched over and engrossed in a large leather-bound tome. Skye's heart sank. In the presence of others, there was no way she would be able to talk to Casey about the cat.

"No problem," Casey said calmly, a mischievous smirk playing on her lips. "Watch this."

Before Skye could protest, Casey stepped forward and raised her hand, curling her fingers as if grasping at an invisible thread. She then muttered a few words under her breath, her voice barely audible even in the silence of the library. Skye watched in anticipation, uncertain of what was happening.

With a flick of her wrist, Casey cast the spell seamlessly. Skye's mouth hung open in awe as the witch at the table slumped forward into her book.

"What did you do?" Skye asked in alarm.

"Don't panic, Skye," Casey said, unperturbed. "It's just a simple sleeping spell."

"I've never seen a spell like that before," said Skye. "Where did you learn it?"

Casey shrugged nonchalantly, her expression unapologetic.

"It's just a little something I picked up from another spell book in the public library in town," she explained, her tone casual. "Soulshade Academy might frown upon spells like this, but I do my own research. I'm not one to blindly follow the rules."

"Will she be ok?" Skye asked, still worried.

"The sleeping spell will wear off before the end of lunch," Casey assured, her certainty unwavering. "She won't remember a thing. It's harmless, Skye. I promise."

As Skye processed Casey's explanation, her mind churned with conflicting thoughts and emotions. On the one hand, she couldn't help but acknowledge the academy's strict policy against spells that altered another person's consciousness. Soulshade's staunch belief in the ethical use of magic was ingrained in every aspect of its teachings, and she respected that. However, as she glanced at the sleeping form of the other witch, a sense of gratitude welled up within her. Casey's unconventional methods had provided them with the privacy they would need for their clandestine conversation to take place.

Ready to listen, Casey took a seat at a single desk. Skye brought another chair to it. As she settled down, ready to talk, she placed her bag on her lap, giving the cat a reassuring pat beneath the purple fabric.

"Due to it being dorm room inspection today, I had no choice but to take the cat with me to class," she began, watching as Casey's brows shot up in surprise. "Something strange happened."

"Oh?"

"He left my bag for a casual stroll around the classroom. Nobody else could see him, Casey!" Skye whispered, her eyes wide with disbelief. "Not even Miss Lumos! He just... walked around the room like he owned the place, and nobody noticed!"

"Wow!" Casey muttered, still processing Skye's revelation. "That's so weird."

"I thought I was going mad," said Skye. "But once I'd managed to calm myself down, I told myself that *you* can see him."

"Exactly," said Casey.

Skye carefully opened the flap on her bag, inviting Casey to take a look inside.

"Yep," Casey said confidently. "I can see him. He's just as vivid and as real as anything else in this room."

"That's a relief," said Skye, her voice trembling a little at the situation. "But why couldn't anyone else see him?"

Casey's expression softened as she took in Skye's obvious distress. She then scratched her head, chewing on her lip as she considered possible explanations.

"There's got to be something special about that cat," she mused. "Something we haven't figured out yet. I'm just as curious as you are. It's definitely worthy of some research."

"Where will you start?" Skye asked.

"That forbidden spell book that I hid down here when we were in detention..." Casey said. "It should still be here."

"It's a long shot," Skye said doubtfully, "but at least it's a start."

"Indeed," said Casey. "I'm willing to bet that if we're dealing with something uncommon here, then the best place to start would be in forbidden literature, if only to ensure that we can rule out anything sinister."

With the cat snoozing contentedly in her bag, Skye left him on the chair. Following Casey's lead, as she ventured deeper into the library, she couldn't help but feel a shiver of excitement mixed with trepidation.

Casey's fingers trailed along the spines of the books as she searched for the forbidden tome. The dust on the shelves seemed to cling to her fingertips, evidence of how rarely anyone ventured into this hidden corner of the academy.

"Here it is," Casey said proudly as she pulled the large book out from its hiding place between other forgotten texts of age. "Exactly where I left it."

With a determined stride, she carried the book back to their desk. Skye followed after her.

"Alright, let's see what we can dig up," Casey

declared as she cracked open the tome with a sense of reverence.

The pages seemed to breathe with power, the cryptic symbols whispering secrets known only to those who dared to tread their elusive paths.

"Casey," Skye said softly. "I really appreciate you doing this. It means a lot to me."

"Hey, no problem," Casey replied, her eyes still on the book as she scanned its contents.

Her fingers tracing the ancient script, Casey scrutinised a small fraction of the book's complex text with a furrowed brow, her lips moving silently as she searched for answers amidst the sea of knowledge contained within. Skye watched in awe, marvelling at the studious witch's depth of expertise as she navigated the arcane text.

After what felt like an eternity, Casey sighed, a hint of frustration creeping into her features.

"It's going to take me a while to find anything useful," she admitted, her tone tinged with disappointment.

As she checked her watch, she sighed again, giving a resigned smile.

"Lunchtime is almost over," she said. "We should head upstairs for our afternoon lessons."

Reluctantly, Skye nodded in agreement, accepting that their time in the underground library was drawing to a close. She watched as Casey carefully placed the book into her bag.

"I'll take this with me," Casey said.

With a sense of purpose, the two witches gathered their belongings, their movements synchronised in a silent rhythm of preparation. Skye carefully put her bag over her shoulder, feeling the weight of her companion nestled within.

As they ascended the stairs up towards ground level, Skye looked admiringly at Casey, appreciative of the older witch's discretion, dedication, and kindness.

Chapter Eleven

Skye hurried down the corridor, her footsteps echoing off the polished floor. The afternoon sunlight streamed in through the tall windows, casting long shadows on the walls. She clutched her bag protectively, grateful that the cat had remained hidden throughout her last lesson of the day.

I wish I'd thought to ask Casey where her dorm room is. I didn't even check to see where she would be for her last class!

Deciding that there was only one way to ease her racing mind, Skye took a deep breath and headed off down the corridor in the direction of her own dorm room. With every step, the weight of the day's events seemed to lift from her shoulders, to be replaced by a growing hope for peace and tranquillity. The bustling energy of the academy began to fade into the background as she focused on the simple pleasure of returning to her own space, where she could unwind and reflect.

As she neared her private sanctuary, she fumbled in her pocket for the key. She could almost feel the tension draining from her body when she looked up to see a piece of paper affixed to her door with masking tape.

Room inspection: passed, she read. *Phew!*

As she unlocked the door and pushed it open, the room appeared untouched. It looked as though whoever had been tasked with carrying out the room inspection had been respectful of her space – so much so that they probably hadn't even thought to look in the drawers, or the cupboard with the bag of hidden cat food at the back.

As soon as she set her bag on the bed, the black cat jumped out, his white paws pressing delicately into the plush mattress. When he stretched his legs, Skye felt a pang of guilt; it was a stark reminder of just how long he had been cooped-up inside. Nevertheless, she couldn't help but smile at his graceful movements, his sleek fur shining in the soft light coming in through the window.

"Hey there," she said, reaching down to stroke him gently as she nodded towards her bag. "I'm sorry you had to stay in there for so long."

The cat purred and rubbed his head against her hand, seeming to understand. Then, reluctantly breaking away from his soft touch, Skye quickly set about filling his food and water bowls.

As she watched him eat, her stomach growled, reminding her that she'd skipped lunch. Rummaging through her drawer, she unearthed a large packet of sweets and a small packet of savoury crackers – not the most nutritious meal, but it would have to do.

"I guess it's dinnertime for both of us," she murmured, tearing open the packets and dumping them onto her bed before settling herself on top of the duvet.

When the cat finished eating, he hopped up onto the bed to be next to Skye, nudging the cracker in her hand with his paw. She laughed and scooted closer to him.

"This is for me, you cheeky thing."

The cat tilted his head in playful defiance.

"Ok," Skye said with a soft chuckle, "you can have some – especially seeing as you asked so nicely."

She smiled as she broke off a piece of cracker for him. As they shared her makeshift meal, she studied the cat, her mind racing with questions. What was it about this creature that made him so special, so invisible to everyone but her and Casey?

"Who are you?" she asked gently, stroking his sleek black fur.

The cat simply purred in response, rubbing his head against her hand. She couldn't help but feel comforted by his presence, despite the enigma he presented. Ever since he'd come into her life, the confusing dream of her mother hadn't returned, and for that alone, Skye loved him.

"Thank you for helping me to sleep better," she whispered, scratching behind the cat's ears. "I don't know how you're doing it, but it means the world to me."

The cat affectionately nuzzled Skye's hand before tilting his head to look up at her. She gazed into his intelligent eyes, searching for understanding, or perhaps even an answer. But the feline only blinked at her, his expression inscrutable.

Barely managing to stifle a yawn, Skye leaned back against the soft pillows, exhaustion weighing her down. The cat curled up beside her, purring soothingly, his black fur blending seamlessly with the dark colours of her uniform. As she gave him another scratch behind the ears, she felt her eyelids growing heavier and heavier, her body begging for rest after such an emotionally draining day. Appreciating the gentle company of her mysterious companion, she soon drifted off into a deep, dreamless sleep that would see her through to the morning.

Chapter Twelve

As the morning sunlight filtered in through the windows of Soulshade Academy, Skye went about her day with a sense of determination and purpose. Her first two lessons had passed by without a hitch. With the cat resting happily in her dorm room instead of being expected to keep still in her bag, it had made all the difference.

All the same though, as much as she had wanted to, Skye hadn't been able to concentrate. She had found herself grappling with a persistent sense of distraction that refused to be ignored. Despite her best efforts to focus on the material being taught, her thoughts kept drifting back to the pressing need to find Casey.

As Skye hurried through the bustling corridors towards her third class of the day, she was hit by a wave of relief when a familiar voice cut through the cacophony of noise around her.

"Skye! Hey, Skye!"

It was Casey. Making her way towards Skye, she weaved through the throng of students with practiced ease.

"Casey!" Skye called back, a smile spreading across her face as she quickened her pace to meet her friend halfway. "I didn't know where you would be today. Thanks for coming to find me."

"Hey, no worries," said Casey. "I went to the notice board to check your class timetable."

"You know what I'm going to ask you," Skye said.

"Indeed," said Casey. "I'm just as keen to talk about it as you are. Shall we meet in the underground library at lunch?"

"Good idea," said Skye.

The two witches headed off in separate

directions to their respective lessons. Skye had no idea what Casey had found, but was appreciative of how the older witch had endeavoured not to talk about their secret in earshot of everyone in the busy corridor.

As Skye settled into her seat for her third lesson of the day, she couldn't shake the feeling of impatience that gnawed at her insides. The minutes stretched on like taffy, each second feeling longer than the last as she struggled to focus on Mrs Perrin's soft voice.

Skye's gaze kept straying to the clock on the wall, the steady tick-tock of its hands echoing in the confines of the classroom. With each glance, her heart sank a little lower, the passing of time only serving to amplify her feeling of restlessness.

Mrs Perrin's voice fluttered on in the background, a distant murmur that seemed to fade in and out of Skye's consciousness. Try as she might to pay attention, her mind kept wandering back to the conversation she'd had with Casey earlier, the promise of answers so tantalisingly out of reach.

That book of Casey's is huge. I hope she was able to find something. Even the smallest bit of information would be helpful.

With each long minute, Skye's impatience grew, her fingers tapping anxiously against the desk as she waited for the lesson to finally come to an end. She longed to escape the confines of the classroom, to break free from the monotony of the lesson and seek out the answers she so desperately craved.

When the bell finally rang to signal the end of the lesson, Skye breathed a sigh of relief, her spirit lifting at the prospect of finally being able to leave the classroom behind. With a sense of urgency, she gathered her belongings and made her way out into the bustling corridor.

With hurried movements, she navigated the familiar corridors until finally, she arrived at the entrance to the underground library. She pushed open the heavy door and stepped inside, the cool air feeling refreshing on her cheeks as she carefully made her way down the steps. As she scanned the dimly lit space before her, she was thankful to observe that there were no other witches around. She smiled to herself, thinking about how there would be no need for Casey to cast any sleep-inducing spells on any poor unsuspecting students.

With the library to herself, Skye took a seat at one of the desks. As much as she tried to, she couldn't quite steady her nerves amidst the anticipation. She casually looked around, taking in the obscure titles of some of the tomes on a nearby shelf.

"Hey, Skye," Casey said in a sing-song voice as she descended the stairs. "Sorry to have kept you waiting. I went to the kiosk en route; I figured that we could do with some sandwiches."

"That's fantastic," Skye said appreciatively, noting that although the musty air wouldn't make for the best environment to eat in, it would be better than going hungry.

"Ok," Casey said, getting straight to the point as she took a seat next to Skye at the small table. "You're not going to like this."

"Oh?" Skye uttered, her voice tarred with worry.

"I spent hours on this. *Hours.* I couldn't find anything. Not even a hint."

Skye couldn't help but feel a sense of defeat wash over her. Over the last twenty-four hours, she had allowed her hope to build.

"Sorry, Skye," Casey said sincerely. "I know it's not what you were hoping for."

"So what now?" Skye asked, her voice edged with frustration.

"I'll give you my honest opinion," Casey said gently, "but you might not like it."

"Go on."

"Well, you know that I generally prefer to find things out for myself. Also, if you would rather keep this whole thing a secret, then you have my word that I will go with you on that. However, the unusual nature of this situation is such that in all honesty, I think you should ask one of the teachers here for their thoughts on the matter."

"I'd rather not," Skye said gravely.

"I know," Casey said kindly, "but at this stage, what's the worst that can happen? The cat is clearly bonded to you. I doubt that anyone here could now claim him for themselves, even if they wanted to. Besides, if anyone tries to, you've got me on your side; I'll happily back you up."

"Thanks, Casey," Skye said, touched by the older witch's loyalty.

A pause hung in the air as Skye weighed up her options.

"Hmm..." she mused. "I suppose out of every teacher I could possibly ask, Miss Lumos would be my first choice. I know she couldn't see the cat, but she's one of the kindest and most knowledgeable teachers here – especially when it comes to the emotional aspects of spirituality and what it is to be a witch."

"I agree," said Casey, her expression a picture of determination. "Would you like me to come with you?"

"Yes, please," Skye enthused. "That would be a big help. Thank you."

"You're welcome," said Casey. "I'm certain that we'll be able to catch Miss Lumos in her office this evening after lessons."

"Right," said Skye, her excitement about the possibility of getting some answers now greater than her fear of revealing their secret. "We'll go and see Miss Lumos this evening."

Chapter Thirteen

The academy's hallways seemed to stretch on endlessly as Skye and Casey made their way towards Miss Lumos' office, their footsteps soft against the wooden flooring. Skye clutched her bag tightly, feeling the comforting presence of the cat inside.

A shiver of anticipation ran down her spine as they drew closer to their destination.

"I'm certain that we're doing the right thing," Casey said, her voice full of conviction as she keenly offered reassurance. "We need answers, and if that means coming clean about the cat, then it will surely be worth it."

Deciding to embrace Casey's perspective, Skye agreed with a nod of her head, clutching her bag tighter. Deep down, she knew that she couldn't keep this secret forever. With everything that had happened over the last few days, she needed answers.

As they reached the ornate wooden door bearing Miss Lumos' nameplate, Skye paused, taking a deep breath to calm her nerves. With one last glance at Casey for encouragement, she raised her hand and knocked cautiously, the sound reverberating through the empty corridor.

"Come in," called a warm, inviting voice from inside.

Skye swallowed hard, her throat suddenly dry as she pushed the heavy door open to be met with the sight of Miss Lumos' office. The cosy room seemed to exude tranquillity.

They hesitated for a moment before stepping inside, feeling as though they were entering into a world far removed from the rest of the academy.

"Hello Skye. Hello Casey," Miss Lumos said, her voice mirroring the welcoming atmosphere of the room. "Do come in."

As they crossed the threshold, Skye couldn't help but marvel at the office's decor. Shelves lined with leather-bound grimoires climbed towards the high ceiling, whilst an assortment of dried herbs and small crystals hung from a wooden rack near the large stained-glass window. A soft, flickering glow emanated from several candles scattered throughout the space, casting dancing shadows on the walls.

At the far end of the room stood a large desk adorned with an array of unusual trinkets – a crystal ball nestled amongst a pile of runes, a brass telescope pointed towards the window, and a small collection of colourful stones arranged into a mesmerising pattern. There was a plush, emerald-green armchair behind the desk, its high back cradling Miss Lumos like a protective shield.

"Take a seat," she said, gesturing at two smaller chairs opposite her desk, her friendly smile putting Skye at ease.

"Thank you," Skye murmured, settling into a chair as Casey did the same.

Skye placed her bag on the floor beside her.

She could feel the cat shifting inside, no doubt curious about the unfamiliar surroundings.

Miss Lumos leaned forward in her chair, her expressive fingers drumming a steady rhythm on the polished wooden surface of her desk.

"How can I help?" she asked, sincerity in her tone.

Skye's heart pounded against her rib cage. There was so much she wanted to say, but the words stuck in her throat like a thick fog. She glanced nervously at Casey, who assertively sat forward to take the lead.

"We've discovered something... unusual," she said frankly, "and we're not sure what to make of it."

"Go on," Miss Lumos urged, her gaze flitting between Skye and Casey.

Skye fiddled with a lose thread on the hem of her dress, her way of silently prompting Casey to elaborate.

"Alright," Casey said, taking a deep breath. "It

all started when we found a cat trapped behind a wall in the underground library during detention."

She paused to gauge Miss Lumos' reaction. Miss Lumos raised an eyebrow, but otherwise remained composed.

"I see," Miss Lumos said thoughtfully. "And what makes this cat so unusual?"

Casey hesitated, casting a quick glance towards Skye before continuing.

"We had to remove some bricks, but we got him out safely. He took a liking to Skye almost immediately," said Casey. "Despite how he must have been trapped behind the wall for goodness knows how long, he was in surprisingly good condition when he came out. It's not just that though: it seems that only Skye and I can see him. So far, he has been invisible to everyone else."

Miss Lumos' eyes widened. She was clearly intrigued.

"Fascinating," she murmured, her gaze darting between the two younger witches. "Tell me more."

"The cat seems to have chosen me, somehow," said Skye, a surge of courage inspiring her to continue the story. "We've been keeping him a secret because we didn't want anyone else to try and claim him as their familiar."

"He has clearly chosen Skye," Casey chimed in, keen to defend their decision.

Miss Lumos' gaze settled on Skye, who suddenly felt self-conscious. She shifted uncomfortably in her seat.

"It's rare for an animal to choose its witch so quickly, particularly under such unusual circumstances," Miss Lumos said, curiously tapping a finger against her chin. "Given your description of how you found him, I can understand your desire to protect him. What does he look like?"

"His fur is mostly black, except for the white marks on his face, his feet, his tummy, and the tip of his tail," Skye said, the words spilling out before she could stop herself. "It's slightly scraggly in places, but he doesn't seem malnourished or anything. And his eyes... they're so intelligent. It's like he understands everything I say. When I was in your class the other day, he actually strolled right out of my bag, bold as anything, and not a single person noticed – even *you* didn't see him!"

Skye hesitated for a moment before carefully bending in her chair to place her bag on her lap. She then slowly opened the flap, causing the appliqué stars to shimmer with the movement.

"Can you see him now, Miss Lumos?" she asked tentatively.

Miss Lumos peered into the bag, her face betraying her inability to see what Skye and Casey could.

"I'm afraid not," she replied gently.

"Oh," Skye uttered, unable to hide her confusion and disappointment as she closed her bag.

"Could it be some sort of spell or enchantment?" Casey asked, desperate for answers. "Or maybe he's not a real cat at all, but some kind of spirit or phantom?"

Skye watched Miss Lumos' face, trying to decipher the teacher's thoughts through the subtle expressions that flitted across her delicate features. The silence seemed to stretch on endlessly, causing Skye to fidget in anticipation.

"Well," Miss Lumos finally said, her voice measured and reflective. "What you're experiencing is quite extraordinary, but not entirely unheard of."

Skye and Casey exchanged glances, relief washing over them at the knowledge that they weren't alone in this bizarre situation.

"Your cat," Miss Lumos continued, "is not a ghost or some kind of spectral being. He exists, just on a different plane than most creatures – one that so far, only you and Casey have managed to perceive."

"Will we always be the only ones who can see him?" Casey asked.

"Not necessarily," Miss Lumos replied. "It is entirely possible that other witches may be able to see him. It all depends on the individual witch."

"Oh," Skye uttered, now struggling to take it all in.

"The spiritual plane on which this particular cat exists is just one of many dimensions that make up our reality," Miss Lumos explained. "It's not uncommon for witches to perceive beings on different planes. It just so happens that you two are seeing this cat on a plane that not many other witches are able to see."

Skye exchanged another glance with Casey, intrigue and excitement mingling between them.

"Your ability to see this cat," Miss Lumos continued, "indicates that you're both tuned-in to the same spiritual dimension – one where the soul of this cat can be seen. He exists within that realm, and has chosen to reveal himself to you."

Feeling a surge of pride and gratitude, Skye cradled her bag close to her chest.

"What if you wanted to see the cat?" Casey asked Miss Lumos. "Or other souls on other dimensions? Couldn't you just do a spell?"

"Yes, Casey, there are spells that could potentially allow me to see the cat," Miss Lumos said, her tone firm. "But to do one would be to alter my own consciousness – something that goes against the ethics of Soulshade Academy, and indeed, my own. We witches must respect the boundaries that exist between different dimensions and spiritual planes. If I'm not meant to see something, then it is for a reason."

Casey nodded thoughtfully, her eyes narrowing as she considered this.

"But don't you feel sad?" she asked. "That you can't see the cat?"

"Of course," said Miss Lumos, a soft smile tugging at the corners of her mouth. "It's natural to feel enthralled or wistful about things we cannot experience. However, I also understand that the universe has its reasons, and I trust in the wisdom of those unseen forces."

Skye couldn't help but admire her teacher's grace and acceptance, even as a slight pang of sadness twisted in her stomach.

"Besides," Miss Lumos added with a playful wink, "I have my own unique abilities and connections. They may not involve cats that are invisible to others, but they bring me joy and fulfilment all the same."

"So I'm not in trouble for wanting to keep the cat as my familiar?" Skye asked cautiously, seeking reassurance.

Miss Lumos chuckled endearingly, shaking her head.

"No, Skye, you are not in trouble. I am incredibly proud of both of you for coming to me with your questions and concerns. It shows great maturity and courage. Besides, I believe this experience has taught you a valuable lesson about the nature of our magical world. Remember: sometimes the most important discoveries come from embracing the unknown and trusting in our instincts."

Along with a newfound sense of gratitude and appreciation for Miss Lumos, relief washed over Skye like a soothing balm.

"Miss Lumos," she said, deciding to be bold. "Can I ask you something personal?"

"Of course, dear," Miss Lumos replied, her voice gentle and encouraging.

"The night before we found the cat, I'd had an upsetting and confusing dream about my mother. She was calling out to me, but I couldn't see her. Although she passed away years ago, the dream was so vivid," Skye confided, her voice raw with emotion. "With the cat sleeping next to me, I've been sleeping better; the dream hasn't returned. Do you think… could it be possible that he came to me because of that?"

Miss Lumos looked at Skye thoughtfully, her expression one of empathy. After a moment of silence, she spoke.

"Skye, the connection between a familiar and their witch can be deeply personal and profound. Whilst I cannot say for certain why the cat entered your life, it is clear that he has brought you comfort and support during a difficult time."

"Is it crazy to think that maybe my mum sent him to me?" Skye asked, desperation tingeing her words.

Miss Lumos gazed into the distance as she contemplated Skye's question. The soft glow of the twilight outside her office window cast a warm, golden light across her face, highlighting the sincerity and wisdom in her gentle approach.

"The ways and movements of every soul is complex and mysterious," she eventually replied, a kindness in her voice. "It is not our place to fully understand it, or to know its intentions. Vitally though, I have no doubt that the cat is drawn to you and that you feel the same way about him. When it comes to the bond between a witch and her familiar, that kind of connection is everything."

Skye bit her lip, disappointment flickering in her eyes. She had been hoping for more certainty, but she understood the limitations.

"Your theory that the cat came into your life because of your dream about your mother is certainly valid, and it would make sense given the circumstances," Miss Lumos added, pausing for a moment to carefully choose her words. "However, there is no witch – myself included – who could definitively confirm whether he was sent to you by your mother or by another spiritual entity entirely."

Skye nodded slowly, absorbing the insight Miss Lumos had offered.

"So can Skye keep the cat?" Casey asked, keen to lift the mood.

"Absolutely," said Miss Lumos, her hands clapping together with enthusiasm. "This mysterious feline has chosen Skye, and I believe he will remain loyal to her for the duration of his natural life, whatever that may be, and regardless of whomever else may or may not be able to see him."

"You should probably name him," Casey said as she turned to address Skye.

The idea caught Skye off guard; she hadn't considered naming him. In the whirlwind of secrecy and confusion surrounding his presence, it simply hadn't crossed her mind.

"Miss Lumos," Skye said in a quiet voice. "I was so afraid that I wouldn't be allowed to keep him."

"Skye, this cat chose you," she said. "You

needn't worry about losing him. It's time to give him a name."

Skye opened the flap of her bag to observe the feline nestled in her lap, his intelligent eyes gazing back at her with intensity. As she took in the wisdom and understanding in his expression, a name came to her in a flash of clarity.

"Maximus! He's called Maximus. That *has* to be his name. I can feel it."

The cat blinked up at Skye, as if acknowledging his name with a silent nod of approval.

"Very well," said Miss Lumos, her voice tinged with pride. "Maximus it is. I shall inform everyone at the staff meeting tomorrow morning. While he may remain invisible to most, it's important that everyone is aware of his presence. After all, we wouldn't want any misunderstandings to occur."

"Too right," said Casey.

"Oh, and that reminds me," said Miss Lumos. "Even if others could see him, no amount of magic or determination could come between Maximus and his chosen witch."

"I bet if Constance and Marissa could see him, they would think otherwise," Skye said, a slight resentment in her tone.

"I understand," Miss Lumos said knowingly. "You have nothing to worry about, Skye. I see how they are with you – and with some of the other students too. They have a long way to go in terms of their empathy towards others – both of them are probably years away from being able to secure a familiar of their own."

"Wow," said Skye. "I guess every witch can only hope to receive the kind of energy that she gives out."

"Exactly," said Miss Lumos, her expression resolute.

"Does Skye still need to keep Maximus a secret to some?" Casey asked.

"No. Those who can't see him will be unaffected by his presence," Miss Lumos explained. "And since he has chosen Skye, he'll always return to her, no matter where he wanders within the academy grounds."

"Are there any other witches here at Soulshade who have invisible familiars like Maximus?" Casey asked.

"Yes," Miss Lumos answered. "There are just two other students and one teacher who have invisible familiars as well. If you'd like, Skye, I can put you in touch with them. It might be helpful to share experiences and advice."

"Yes, please," Skye enthused. "That would be amazing. Thank you."

"Considering the hundreds of witches at Soulshade Academy, it's fascinating to think how rare something like this must be," Casey remarked.

"Indeed," Miss Lumos agreed wisely. "Invisible familiars are quite rare, which makes your bond with Maximus all the more special, Skye. Cherish and nurture it, for it will only grow stronger over time."

Skye felt a surge of happiness at hearing this. She hadn't been going mad. She wasn't in trouble. Maximus was hers and he was here to stay. Free from the confines of secrecy, he could now roam the grounds of Soulshade Academy. Not only that, but no longer burdened by the fear of discovery, Skye could finally embrace the bond they shared without reservation.

Chapter Fourteen

Several weeks later, beneath a bright, slightly overcast sky, Skye and Casey met up for lunch on a wooden bench in one of the academy's many recreational courtyards. Enjoying the lush grass beneath him, Maximus lay curled up at their feet, his eyes half-closed in contentment.

"It's nice to finally be able to enjoy lunch together like this," Skye said as she glanced down at Maximus. "We no longer have to worry about keeping him a secret."

"Definitely," Casey agreed, taking a bite of her sandwich. "Even though others can't see him, I'm so glad that everyone's accepted Maximus as your familiar."

Skye looked around, admiring the tranquillity of the academy grounds.

Students strolled along the cobblestone paths, some chatting animatedly while others buried their noses in books. A gentle breeze rustled the leaves of the ancient oaks that stood sentinel over the manicured lawns. The scent from the nearby flowerbeds filled the air, sweet and soothing.

"Thanks for sticking by me throughout all of this," she said to Casey. "The last few weeks have been fantastic. Miss Lumos was right. I've been a lot calmer now that I know Maximus is officially mine and no longer has to be kept a secret."

"You're welcome," said Casey, sincerity in her tone. "I'm just happy I could help. Besides, I've loved learning about the nature of invisible familiars. It's fascinating stuff. I might even study it for my dissertation next year."

Skye smiled, pleased that Casey was enjoying her studies.

"Maybe now you won't have to seek out extra reading in forbidden texts from the public library," she teased gently.

"Hey!" Casey retorted playfully, a grin spreading across her face. "You know me – I'll always be curious. Besides, if it wasn't for that forbidden spell book and my detention with you in the underground library, perhaps we wouldn't have found Maximus behind that wall."

"Good point," Skye said, smiling fondly at the memory.

"I've been meaning to ask," said Casey, "have you had any more upsetting dreams about your mum since you've had Maximus?"

"I haven't," said Skye, her relief evident. "I mean, I've had dreams about her, but they've all been... nice. Not distressing at all."

"That's amazing! Do you think it has anything to do with Maximus sleeping on your bed?"

"Maybe," Skye mused, reaching down to trail her fingers along Maximus' fur. "It's like he's brought a sense of peace into my life."

"It sounds like he's doing an excellent job as a familiar, then," Casey said happily, glancing down at the relaxed feline.

"Speaking of sleep," said Skye, "now that I don't have to keep Maximus a secret anymore, I bought him a cat bed. I put it in the corner of my dorm room. He doesn't bother with it though. He prefers to sleep on my bed."

"It just goes to show that he is truly kind, protective, and loyal," said Casey. "Everything a good familiar should be."

As it neared the end of lunchtime, Skye spotted Miss Lumos walking across the courtyard. With a pile of books in her arms, she seemed to be en route to her next class.

"Hello Skye. Hello Casey," she called out to them. "Give Maximus a little scratch behind the ears for me, won't you?"

"Of course," said Skye, cheerfully reaching down to pet Maximus. "There you go, Maximus. That's from Miss Lumos."

"Thank you, Skye," Miss Lumos replied, her voice filled with an endearing warmth.

With a friendly wave, the helpful teacher then bid farewell to the conversation. As she headed towards her destination, she adjusted her grip on the books in her hands to ensure that not a single tome would slip from her grasp.

"She's brilliant," Casey said as they watched Miss Lumos walk away. "I'm with her for my last lesson of the day. I'd better get moving."

"Ok," said Skye. "See you again soon."

Her gaze lingered on Casey's retreating figure as the older witch made her way to class. Then, with a graceful movement, Skye reached down to lift Maximus onto her lap. She couldn't help but marvel at the strange and wonderful path that had led her to this moment.

Together, they sat in a companionable silence, the world around them fading into the background as they basked in the soothing comfort of each other's presence.